THE CASE OF THE
WANTED MAN

Anne Schraff

PAGETURNERS

DETECTIVE

The Case of the Bad Seed
The Case of the Cursed Chalet
The Case of the Dead Duck
The Case of the Wanted Man
The Case of the Watery Grave

SCIENCE FICTION
Bugged!
Escape From Earth
Flashback
Murray's Nightmare
Under Siege

SPY
A Deadly Game
An Eye for an Eye
I Spy, e-Spy
Scavenger Hunt
Tuesday Raven

ADVENTURE
A Horse Called
   Courage
Planet Doom
The Terrible Orchid Sky
Up Rattler Mountain
Who Has Seen the
   Beast?

MYSTERY
The Hunter
Once Upon a Crime
Whatever Happened
   to Megan Marie?
When Sleeping Dogs
   Awaken
Where's Dudley?

Development and Production: Laurel Associates, Inc.
Cover Illustrator: Black Eagle Productions

SADDLEBACK
PUBLISHING • INC.
Three Watson
Irvine, CA 92618-2767
E-Mail: info@sdlback.com
Website: www.sdlback.com

ISBN 1-56254-389-X

CONTENTS

Chapter 1

"He's making my life a nightmare!" April Foster said as she took her seat next to Rollie Torres' desk. At 23 years old, Rollie was working part-time at Raven Investigation Services. The firm specialized in marital shadowing and searches for assets and missing persons. They also did background checks on prospective employees. This job looked like something quite a bit different. According to her story, local aspiring actress and model April Foster was being hounded by a would-be suitor.

"Every time I turn around—whether I'm at the supermarket, the bank, or the movies—there he is, leering at me!" she complained.

Rollie was still taking criminal justice

classes in college. He hoped to enter the Police Academy class next spring.

"You know, Ms. Foster, this really isn't our line, dealing with stalkers. I think you may need to go to the police with this one," Rollie said.

He studied the young woman sitting before him. April was a beautiful girl with huge dark eyes and pouty cherry lips. She had an incredible figure. All of a sudden she leaned forward and stared hard at Rollie. "Don't I know you?" she asked. "You look so familiar!"

Rollie shook his head. "I don't think so," he said. No way he'd have forgotten a girl this gorgeous. But somehow she *did* look vaguely familiar. Maybe it was something about her eyes. . . .

"What's your name?" April asked, looking a bit embarrassed. "When that guy pointed me toward your desk, he must have mentioned your name. But I guess I didn't pay any attention to it. That cranky old man at the front desk was kind of mumbling anyway."

The "cranky old man" was Rollie's boss, a tough, 50-year-old ex-cop named Rene Dumas.

"Then let me introduce myself. My name is Roland Torres, but everyone calls me Rollie," Rollie said pleasantly.

"*Yes!*" April almost screamed. "You were in Ms. Bradley's civics class at Wilson High School, about six years ago!"

"Yeah, I was there all right." Rollie was bewildered, but then it came to him. Those big fawn eyes staring at him belonged to chubby Margaret Fierster! She had been the fat girl—the target of every sophomore guy's "dog" jokes. Sometimes guys would walk behind her, mocking her waddle. While Rollie himself didn't make any ugly jokes about Margaret, he sure had laughed along with his buddies. Remembering that now made him feel ashamed.

What in the world had happened? How had pathetic Margaret Fierster ever turned out to be this beautiful creature called April Foster?

"*Margaret?*" he gasped when he caught his breath.

"Uh-huh," April said proudly. "As you see, I got rid of all those pounds—and look what was hiding underneath!"

"Wow, you sure—I mean, you look *great*!" Rollie sputtered.

"Rollie, did you have any idea that I had a major crush on you back then? I thought you were the handsomest boy in school. Why, I'd just stare at your picture in the yearbook for hours and hours," April gushed.

"Uh, no—I never knew that," Rollie said, feeling a little uncomfortable. He felt a wave of guilt, too. Margaret—or April—she *had* to have seen him snickering at some of those fat jokes. But maybe she didn't remember. After all, it *was* six years ago.

"Well," April said, "getting back to my problem. You just said I should go to the police about it. But I already have—and they were no help at all. They didn't take me seriously. They *said* they investigated—but they couldn't find anybody stalking me! It just made me furious. This guy is so clever. He sneaked into the theater when I was rehearsing for *West Side Story* down at Borley Auditorium. I had a small part in that show. Anyway, he was there several times, just hanging around and staring at me. It made my skin crawl."

"Well, have you any idea who this guy is? Did you ever talk to him at all?" Rollie asked.

"No, he's just always watching me, *leering* at me. I think I've become the focus of his sick life. And do you know what he does? He always carries this silk handkerchief. Red silk. When he sees I'm watching, he ties it in a knot. Then he yanks on it, tightening the knot, and then he laughs. I'm so terrified. It's like—you know—he plans to *strangle* me!" April cried. "Oh, Rollie, I really need your help!"

"Well, let me see," Rollie said. He got up from his chair. "Wait here. I'll talk to my boss and see what we can do."

"*Please* help me, Rollie," April said. "I'm desperate!"

Rollie pulled up a chair at Mr. Dumas' desk. He told him the whole story. "I'd like to take on this stalking case, Mr. Dumas. The girl really seems distraught," Rollie said.

"That dippy little actress?" Rene Dumas snorted. "I don't believe a word of her story. She tell you about the stalker with the red silk handkerchief? Yeah, *right*! But if she's got the money— sure, we'll give it a shot. Why not? It'd be good experience for you, Rollie."

Rollie returned to his desk, where April waited. "It's all set. We'll try to help you," he said.

"Oh, Rollie, thank you! You don't know how much this means to me! I haven't been able to sleep nights. I can hardly perform, knowing he's out there somewhere waiting for me," April said.

"So, can you give me a description of this guy?" Rollie asked.

"Yes. He's very tall—about six foot two or three inches. He weighs about 145. He's gaunt, you know—not well-built like you are," April said. "How much do *you* weigh, Rollie?"

"About 170," Rollie said.

"I thought something like that. But this guy, he's your height but much skinnier. Oh, and he has these narrow little eyes, like a snake's eyes. Just slits, really. It's like his eyes are never really open all the way. And he's got this long nose and sort of a receding chin," April said, her voice filling with revulsion. "He's *gross*, Rollie, really gross."

"How old would you say this man is?" Rollie asked.

"Maybe 40. I wouldn't be surprised if he's one of those dangerous 'loner' types. I bet he's never even had a *real* girlfriend, so he's built a fantasy about me in his sick little mind. Just before all this started, I got this really weird phone call—and I think it was from him. A horrible raspy voice asked me if I ever date fans. I told him no—absolutely not. Then he goes, 'You better date *me* if you know what's good for you.' And then he hung up," April said, shuddering.

Rollie noticed that she was wearing a tight pink pullover sweater and even tighter jeans. Her figure was dynamite. She surely had enough going for her to stir up some love-starved weirdo. If April had looked like this at Wilson High, the guys would have been climbing the lockers for a date with her.

"Do you have any idea how the guy got your phone number?" Rollie asked.

"Some jerk at the theater where I was doing this little experimental play. We all listed our addresses and phone numbers when we were hired. I think this jerk gave out the information by mistake," April said. "Actually, I went out with the guy a few times. He got really steamed when I wasn't interested in a relationship with him. So he might have given out my phone number just out of revenge."

"What's his name?" Rollie asked.

"Oh, he has nothing to do with the guy who's stalking me," April said. "I don't even know what his address is. He's probably not in town anymore. His name is Danny Jones—but like I said, he's not involved in the stalking."

Rollie nodded. "You never know. He might have some more information about the guy he gave your number to. Okay, then—uh—April, when does this stalker usually show up?"

"He used to come regularly to my performances, but our show closed last night. I'm between jobs now. I expect to get another acting or dancing job real soon. But sometimes he also hangs out on the street across from my apartment building. That really scares me. I can't help being afraid that he'll break in or something," April said.

Rollie tried to be reassuring. "He's probably just a harmless nut. Most of these guys are. But there's always the exception, of course—so we've got to take it seriously. Don't worry. We'll find him and tell him that stalking is a crime, and that he's got to knock it off. Then if he continues to bother you, we'll get a restraining order from the police. Stalking is no joke anymore—not with the tough new laws."

"Oh, Rollie, I just feel so much safer now that I have your help," April said. "You know, over the years I've been keeping up on you. I've kept in touch with friends from our class. That's how I knew you were still attending college when you got this job. Don't laugh when I tell you this: Even though you and I never dated, in my heart you were my first boyfriend! Is that silly or what?"

Rollie smiled at April and said, "Well, I'll get on this right away."

"Then you'll be staying pretty close to me, right, Rollie? This creep has followed me even when I was out on a date. Maybe it would be a good idea if you and I went to dinner sometimes. What do you think? Then you could see him with your own eyes."

Chapter 2

Rollie was amazed. "You mean this guy is so bold that he shows up when you're with somebody else?" he asked.

"Yes, it's like he wants to show me that he's unstoppable. He wants me to know that he can terrorize me at will, and I'm *helpless* to do anything about it!" April said, her voice rising.

"Well, now this guy's got a new problem—me," Rollie said, "and he's about to find out that stalkers get lost fast—*or* they get to wear prison clothes for a long time."

April touched Rollie's arm. "How about us getting together for dinner tonight at Rovers?" she said sweetly. "It's that barbecue place off I-18. The stalker has already followed me there several times. Rovers might be just the place to trap him."

Usually, Rollie spent his Friday nights with his girlfriend, Vivian Garcia. But Vivian would understand if he was needed on the job. And it did seem like a pretty good idea. Maybe he could trap the stalker right away. "Okay," Rollie said. "I'll pick you up around seven. Then we'll just hope this creep shows up at Rovers."

"Oh, that's terrific, Rollie. It's a big load off my mind," April said.

April Foster walked out of the office then. As Rollie watched her go, he was still marveling at the change in Margaret Fierster. He slowly shook his head, remembering how she could barely fit in the desk seat, how the boys would nudge each other and make crude remarks. Who would have believed there was a stunning beauty hidden beneath all those extra pounds?

When Rollie got home he called one

of the high school buddies he still kept up with. David Spencer was also heading for a career in the justice system. He was going into the U.S. Border Patrol. Rollie and David often went fishing together or rode their motorbikes into Baja California. David was already engaged to be married to his long-time girlfriend. But Rollie and Vivian hadn't gotten that far yet. Still, Rollie figured that he and Vivian would probably get married once he had a secure job with the police department.

"Hey, Dave, listen up. You'll never believe who came into the office today—Margaret Fierster!" Rollie said.

"You're *kidding* me, man! I'll bet she weighs at least three hundred pounds by now," David laughed.

"No, listen—she's the most beautiful girl I ever saw! It's absolutely amazing, Dave. She weighs about 120 pounds, if that. And not only is she terrific looking, she's an *actress*. I'm telling you the truth,

Dave, she's one hot babe," Rollie said.

"Margaret Fierster?" David cried.

"I'm not kidding, buddy. She calls herself April Foster now. She came into the agency today with a story about some guy stalking her. She thinks it's a lovesick idiot who saw her in a play and started to fantasize about her. I'm telling you, man, a guy would have no trouble building a fantasy about a girl like that. Since I'm working the case, I'm having dinner with her tonight," Rollie said.

"Well, you lucky dog!" David said. "Doesn't Vivian mind?"

"Nah, I just called her and explained that I had to work tonight. She was okay with it. I never talk to Vivian about the investigation work we do. That would be unprofessional. We get into a lot of personal data about people, and it wouldn't be right to talk to outsiders about it," Rollie said.

"In other words, Vivian thinks you're holed up in your office tonight, going over boring crime reports. She has no idea you're dining with a hot babe, right?" David asked.

Rollie was irritated by David's teasing, but he tried to laugh it off. "Come on," he said, "it's a job!"

When Rollie got home later he dug out his old high school yearbooks. He hadn't looked at them in ages, but now he turned quickly to the photo of Margaret Fierster. And there she was, a sad smile on her chubby face. But he saw that even then her eyes were lovely—almost magical. It was sad that everybody was so busy ridiculing Margaret for her weight that no one noticed her wonderful eyes!

Rollie took a closer look at the picture. Underneath the students' names were little blurbs about them—sayings they had chosen, a line of poetry, or a list of their school activities. Beneath Margaret's picture was just one word—*crosswords*. Rollie vaguely remembered that now. Margaret had spent her entire high school career doing crossword puzzles in her spare time. She had plenty of spare time, too—because she was shunned from parties, and as far as he knew she never had a single date.

Now Rollie felt funny about his conversation with his girlfriend. Maybe he should have told Vivian that he was working on a case that required him to take his client to dinner. Vivian wasn't a jealous person, but Rovers was a popular hangout for a lot of twenty-somethings. If someone told her he was there, she would be hurt. Rollie had to admit that he would be upset if the tables were turned. If Vivian hadn't told him that she was having a business dinner with some good-looking young dude, he'd be plenty steamed. But Rollie figured that the odds were with him. Vivian wasn't likely to find out. Maybe the lovesick weirdo who was stalking April would show his hand quickly.

Then the case would be over, and he would never see April again.

Rovers was a middle-class sports bar that catered to younger people by featuring hot new music. Rollie picked April up at her apartment and drove the few blocks to the restaurant. They walked in together.

"Let's take a table that's out in the open," Rollie suggested. "If the stalker is lurking anywhere around, I want him to see you and make his move. Then I've got him."

"Okay," April said. A moment later she was glancing at the menu. "I usually order just a green salad and a little wine. I have to watch my diet like a hawk," she giggled.

Rollie ordered a cheeseburger. He kept his eyes on the door, looking for the man April had described.

"So, Rollie—you want to be a police officer, huh?" April asked as she sipped ice water.

"Yeah, but how did you find that out?" Rollie asked.

"I told you I've been checking up on you. I've got my sources. I was dirt to the boys, but I had a few nice girlfriends who stuck with me. I'll tell you one thing, Rollie—you'll be the handsomest cop *I* ever saw."

"I don't know about that," Rollie said self-consciously. "I enjoy the classes I'm taking in criminal justice, and I think I can be a good cop."

"Is your girlfriend somebody we went to school with?" April asked.

"So you know about my girlfriend, too? I'm impressed, April. Maybe *you're* the one who should be a detective!" Rollie said wryly.

"You really had a lot of girlfriends at Wilson. Why, you must have dated every cheerleader. Oh, how I envied those little dolls in their skimpy little outfits. Half the time I wanted to *kill* them!" April laughed. "I don't remember you ever dating a girl named Vivian Garcia, though. Did she even go to Wilson?"

Again, Rollie was surprised. How did April know Vivian's name?

"No, I didn't know Vivian in high school. We met at college. She's studying to be an elementary school teacher."

The waiter brought their food, and the stalker had not yet shown up. April started talking about how she had lost so much weight. She described how she had dieted and exercised, and then followed a strict daily regimen to keep the weight off. "I was into all kinds of wild diets for a while. My weight shot up and down like a yo-yo. But then, about two years ago, I found just the right combination of dieting and fitness training. *Finally*, the pounds dropped off and stayed off! It's easier now. I'm not even tempted to eat that junk food I used to live on."

Suddenly, as Rollie was putting extra

sauce on his cheeseburger, April's eyes widened. "He's out there now!" she gasped. "He just peeked in the door!"

"Okay, be cool," Rollie said quickly. "I'll pretend that I'm going to the restroom. Then I'll duck out the back door and come around to the front. That should surprise him. You stay right here, April. You're safe where you are. With all of these people around, he wouldn't dare do anything. So, tell me, how is the guy dressed?"

"Like always. Black sweatshirt, black jogging pants," April said.

Rollie got up slowly as if he had nothing more serious on his mind than going to the restroom. If the creep was peering in one of the windows, Rollie didn't want him to be spooked. Then Rollie hurried out the back door and sprinted along the side of the building, coming out in front.

The front area was well-lighted. The only man Rollie saw was an elderly gentleman in a walker being assisted by his wife. Maybe, Rollie thought, the guy had lost his nerve when he saw how crowded the place was. Or maybe seeing April with a big, muscular guy like Rollie had suddenly changed his plans.

Rollie stood around for a few minutes, scanning the surrounding area. But there was nothing to see, so he went back inside Rovers.

"I guess he got scared. He must have taken off before I got there, April," Rollie said.

"Didn't you see him *at all*?" April asked frantically.

"No, I'm afraid not," Rollie said.

April covered her face with her hands and began to cry.

Chapter 3

"Hey, April," Rollie said, reaching over to pat her shoulder. "Take it easy. We'll get the guy—I promise you! Then you'll be able to get on with your life."

April smiled a little and patted her tears with a tissue. "Your girlfriend is so lucky to have a guy like you. Does she know how lucky she is?" she asked.

"Oh, I've got my share of faults," Rollie said. "We all do. There are no perfect people, you know. Vivian knows all about my flaws."

"What a pretty name—*Vivian*," April said. "It's kind of old-fashioned, isn't it? You rarely hear that name anymore."

"Vivian and I are both Hispanics. We don't go with the trendy names as much as some other people do. Vivian had several ancestors with that name, you know? My grandfather's name is Roland, too. The Garcia and Torres families are crawling with Vivians and Beatrices and Rolands," Rollie said.

April picked at her salad without eating much. Rollie felt sorry for her. The price of staying fashionably thin was apparently never eating a full meal.

As they drove back to April's apartment, Rollie said, "I'm glad you have good security at your building. I like those places where a stranger can't just walk in off the street."

"Yeah," April said with little interest. "Will you call me tomorrow?"

"Sure thing. You can give me your schedule, and I'll try to stay pretty close. I want to nab that jerk as soon as possible," Rollie said.

"Does your girlfriend live real close to your place?" April asked.

"No, she lives in one of the dorms on campus," Rollie said.

"Oh, that's nice. I never went to college. But I always thought it would be fun to live in a dorm and belong to a sorority and stuff like that," April said.

Rollie dropped April at her door and drove home. April was probably right. The stalker must be a desperately lonely man who could only fantasize about being with a beautiful girl. But he *could* be dangerous. Rollie remembered the guy who stalked and killed a TV sitcom actress, and the nutcase who had gunned down John Lennon.

When Rollie got home he called David, whose father was a police detective. "See what you can find out about the police report April filed," Rollie asked. "She said the police investigated, but couldn't find anything. But maybe there's something in that report that I could use."

David called back in the morning. "There never was a police report filed," he told Rollie.

"Really? Well, she *said* the police didn't take her seriously. But I thought that they'd at least write up a routine report," Rollie said.

The moment Rollie said goodbye to David, the phone rang again. It was Vivian. "Hi, Rollie," she said. "How are things? I missed our date last night. Did you get all your work done?"

"Yeah, I was pretty busy," Rollie said. He was still feeling guilty that he hadn't been totally honest with her. But after all—he was protecting a client. It wasn't like he had gone out with another girl for *fun*.

"It must be boring to be stuck in the office on a Friday night," Vivian said. Now Rollie was nervous. Vivian's voice didn't sound right. Was she suspicious? Or was it just his imagination working overtime?

"Yeah, sure. Hey, I can't wait to see you. Are we still on for the jazz concert on Sunday afternoon, Viv?" Rollie asked.

"I don't know," Vivian said flatly.

"How come? We've been planning to go for two weeks," Rollie said.

"Well maybe you'd rather take that gorgeous girl you were with at Rovers last night! I mean, who could blame you? I'm just a college girl training to be a school teacher. That's pretty tame stuff compared to a slinky actress," Vivian said, sounding hurt and angry at the same time.

"Whoa, Vivian! That was a client of our detective agency. She's being stalked by some creep. I went with her in the hopes of drawing the stalker out of the shadows," Rollie explained.

"Is that right?" Vivian snapped. "You were assigned to spend as much time as possible with a beautiful little actress to protect her from some bad guy? That sure sounds like an interesting case. I wonder why you didn't bother to tell me about it, Rollie."

"Vivi, I'm sorry! I guess I *should* have

told you, but I didn't want you to worry. You know, I usually work on boring background checks and stuff like that. But there's an element of risk in this case. And I didn't want you to get upset," Rollie said. But he knew that was only a half-truth. The fact was that he didn't want Vivian to know he'd be spending so much time with such a gorgeous girl.

"Maybe you just wanted to keep your new little friend a secret, Rollie, so you could enjoy her company for a while," Vivian said sharply. Rollie had never seen the jealous side of Vivian's personality. He was surprised that she remained angry even after he had explained that it was all part of his job.

"Vivian, I've got a job to do. You're a smart girl. You know that men and women get thrown together in the working world all the time. Are you going to have a fit of jealousy every time I happen to work alongside a female?

Think about it, Vivian—once I become a cop, my partner might be a woman. She might be *beautiful*! Would you want me to quit the police department then?" Rollie said.

"Usually, people aren't cuddling and kissing with their clients!" Vivian yelled. Rollie could tell she was crying now.

"Vivian, whoever told you anything like that is a rotten *liar*!" Rollie shouted into the phone. "Who said that, anyway? One of your catty little girlfriends who likes to dish the dirt so much? How come you hang out with such no-brain creeps? Do you really feel comfortable with girls who like to spread evil, lying gossip?"

"Never mind who told me," Vivian said, her voice trembling. "You *cheated* on me, Rollie—and I thought we had a commitment to each other! You lied to me about having to work so you could spend the night fooling around with some wannabe actress in a singles bar!

Well, I'm *glad* I found out, Rollie, before it's too late! I don't want to waste my time with a guy who can't be trusted."

"Well, that's just *great*, Viv!" Rollie said sarcastically. "After all we've meant to each other! If you're going to believe a lie like that without even listening to my side of the story, then I don't want to waste my time on *you*, either!"

Vivian banged down the phone.

Rollie groaned and flopped down on the couch. With a sigh of frustration, he buried his face in his hands. He should have known that one of Vivian's stupid girlfriends would be at Rovers. Isn't that the way things happen? You only run into somebody you know when that's the *last* thing you need at the moment! It doesn't matter if you've been pure as the driven snow for 364 days of the year. Just screw up *one* day—and that's the day your grandparents and four people from the church are standing around watching you!

"She's a jealous, possessive woman," Rollie said to himself. But even as those words formed in his mind, the thought shocked him. Vivian had always seemed so rational and well-balanced! Now, when the chips were down, was she really showing her true nature?

But there was a nagging doubt in Rollie's mind. In Vivian's place, maybe *he* would have reacted in the same way. If Dave said he'd seen Vivian in a romantic clutch with some other dude, he might be acting worse than she was.

But what kind of a friend would lie like that?

Rollie decided to shrug the whole thing off for the time being. He called April to plan the day's activities. Even though his personal life was in shambles, he had to solve this case.

"Oh, Rollie, thanks for calling. I'm going down to the auditorium for an audition this afternoon. I'll be there around four. Maybe you could come, too—in case the stalker shows up. I've seen him hanging around there before," April said.

"Okay. It's the Civic Auditorium on Fifth Street, right?" Rollie asked.

"Yes, it is. You're a doll, Rollie," April said, sounding relieved. "I'm already pretty nervous about my audition. It's too much to have this stalker to worry about, too."

"Well, now you can concentrate on the audition. I'll take care of the stalker," Rollie assured her.

When Rollie hung up, he stared at the framed picture of Vivian on his computer table. She was a pretty girl with short, curly hair and dark, wide-set eyes. Nobody would call her *gorgeous*, he supposed—but she suited Rollie just fine. And he really did care deeply about her. She had been a big, important part of his life for a long time—and now he felt empty. This was *impossible*. He had begun to take it for granted that he and

Vivi would be married one day.

Rollie was stunned. How could it all have come apart so quickly? And all because of a stupid lie!

Chapter 4

The downtown auditorium was large and well-lit. Today's audition, or "cattle call," was for a new musical production called *Cross Currents*. April had told him that she was primarily an actress, but that she could also dance. That's what she would be doing if she got the part she was after. The story was about a group of ballerinas trying to juggle their professional and personal lives. The lead role was a talented girl named Vera. That was the part April was going for.

Rollie sat in the front row. When they had come in, April had explained to the producers that he was a close friend. She didn't dare spook them by saying he was a detective. It would be a big mistake, she said, to let anyone know that somebody was stalking her. What producer would want to hire a girl in *that* kind of trouble?

Rollie watched April dance a lively jazz number. She looked terrific in her red costume. Without question, she was the most beautiful girl trying out for the lead—but she wasn't the best dancer. In fact she wasn't even a very *good* dancer. But Rollie enjoyed watching her anyway. He kept thinking about the old days when she was poor Margaret Fierster. Back then, absolutely nobody—including Rollie—would have given her the time of day.

After the audition, April rushed to Rollie's side and breathlessly told him she was getting a "callback." That meant the producers were definitely interested in her—if not for the lead, then for some supporting role.

"That's great," Rollie said, as he walked her to her car. She had a little MG, very old but lovingly polished. But when she reached out for the door handle April let out a piercing shriek.

Rollie glanced up and saw the red silk handkerchief knotted on her aerial. "Oh, Rollie!" April cried. "He was *here*!"

"Take it easy," Rollie said. "It's okay. I'm here with you."

April started to cry, her shoulders convulsing. Rollie put his arm around her and tried to comfort her. "How does he find me?" she sobbed. "Oh, Rollie, he must be lurking close by all the time, watching me. Oh, I could just die!"

Rollie stared up at the tall buildings around the auditorium. He wondered if the guy could be standing behind one of those windows right now, looking down on them.

"Rollie, I'm so frightened!" April said. "Will you follow me home and make sure that I get inside all right?"

"Sure, I'll be right behind you until you're safe," Rollie promised.

Rollie grabbed a plastic bag from his

glove compartment and pulled the red silk handkerchief off the aerial. Then he slipped it into the bag and sealed it. Probably it wouldn't lead to the stalker, but anything was possible. You never knew when you might get lucky. Maybe it was an unusual handkerchief from some little specialty store. Maybe the store clerk would remember a creepy-looking skinny guy who bought a whole bunch of red silk handkerchiefs.

When they got to April's apartment, she begged Rollie to come inside for a cup of coffee. "Just stay with me for a few minutes until I calm down," she pleaded.

Sitting down on the sofa, Rollie sipped his coffee and looked around the living room. It was pleasantly furnished, but it wasn't hard to tell that April didn't have a lot of money. There weren't any expensive paintings or other fancy decorations.

"I have a surprise for you, Rollie. Just

give me a minute. This is something you'll get a big kick out of," April said. She disappeared briefly into her bedroom and then returned with the Wilson High yearbook. She sat beside Rollie on the sofa and flipped to his senior picture. Rollie had been voted *Most Adorable Senior Boy,* and those words had been printed under his picture.

Rollie was embarrassed. At the time it had been great fun, of course. But he was surprised to see what April had done with the picture. She had glued a lacy valentine border all around it! And she'd pasted love poems all over the page, covering the faces of some of the other kids. A cut-out red heart next to his picture had the names *Rollie & Maggie* written on it.

Now April smiled at Rollie and said, "I already admitted that I was crazy in love with you, didn't I? Can you believe it? Me—Margaret Fierster—the most abused fat girl in the history of Wilson

High. I was actually in love with the most gloriously handsome boy in the whole school. Is that a scream or what?"

Chapter 5

Rollie didn't know what to say. A weak "Wow!" slipped from his lips. He was feeling very uncomfortable. "Well, that's very flattering. But we were just kids then. When you're sixteen or seventeen, *everything* in life seems so deadly serious, doesn't it?"

"Will you tell me something I've always wanted to know, Rollie? Who were *you* in love with back then?" April asked. "It was Jenny Baldwin, right?"

Rollie shrugged and said, "Oh, I liked Jenny all right. We went together for a little while. Maybe I even *thought* we were in love. But when you're sixteen, real love is a joke."

In the years since high school, Rollie had come to see that a person had to be mature in order to have a mature love relationship. Now he thought about Vivian. He wanted to rush over to the college campus right now and patch things up with her somehow. He felt miserable. He didn't want this ugly bitterness between them to go on any longer. He knew that he loved Vivian. It scared him to think that losing her was a distinct possibility.

April was giggling when she flipped to Jenny's picture. "Look what I did back then! Wasn't I *bad*?" she laughed.

Jenny Baldwin was a pretty girl, but you would never know it once Margaret Fierster had gotten through with her picture. Margaret had covered Jenny's light blond hair with purple corkscrew curls. Then she'd drawn dark, heavy-rimmed glasses and put a patch on her right eye. She'd drawn black wrinkle lines all over Jenny's lovely face and put a big red pimple in the middle of her perfect little nose. She'd made pretty

Jenny look like a hideous old witch.

Rollie tried to laugh it off. "Boy, April, you were mad at her, huh?"

"I was *so* jealous," April admitted. "You can't imagine! Here was this big hippo who couldn't even get a date with an *ugly* boy. Yet, I was after the best-looking guy at Wilson and hating the girl who had him. Oh, yeah—I was frustrated out of my mind. I even thought of *poisoning* Jenny. Isn't that awful? I dreamed that you might notice me if—if she died. Is that weird or what? Of course I know better now. If something had happened to Jenny, you still wouldn't even have thrown me a crumb. You'd have gone after some other beauty."

Rollie shrugged. He got up and looked out the window. April had said that she'd seen the stalker hanging around her apartment. Rollie wished the guy would show himself now—right down there under the streetlights. Then

Rollie could wrap this thing up. As pretty as April was, Rollie didn't want to spend more time with her. She made him nervous. He felt *awful* about Vivian. Some way or another, he had to fix things up between them. He desperately wanted to get things back to normal.

"Well, I don't see anybody down there," Rollie said, "so I better be going."

"I wish you didn't have to go right away," April said.

"Don't worry. I'll check in with you in the morning," Rollie said, edging toward the door.

"I feel so safe when you're here," April said forlornly.

"You *are* safe here. This is a secure building," Rollie said.

"You know, Rollie, it's too bad that you've got a steady girlfriend," April said. "Because if you didn't, then maybe you and I would hit it off. I mean—look at me. I'm not Margaret Fierster anymore, you know."

Then Rollie felt foolish. It finally dawned on him that April's feelings for him had not changed since she was dumpy Margaret Fierster.

"No, you sure aren't her. You're truly a beautiful girl, April," Rollie said. "I'm sure you have no problem getting dates now, right?"

"No, I don't. But none of those guys are *you*, Rollie," April said sadly. "Don't you believe that it's *possible* to find true love in high school? Just because you're fifteen or sixteen doesn't mean that you can't recognize your one true love!"

"Puppy love doesn't last," Rollie said. "That just happens in the movies. We don't even know who we are when we're kids." He hurried toward the door.

"Just what I need," Rollie thought to himself. "A lovesick client and a jealous girlfriend!"

Rollie was shocked when April followed him to the door and put her arms around him. "Just hold me tight this one time," she pleaded. "What would it hurt to just give me one little hug for good luck!"

Rollie's arms were pinned to his sides. "Take it easy, April. High school was a long time ago. I'll be in touch with you soon. I can see that you're under a lot of stress—but everything will be okay, I promise you!" Rollie said. Then he ran out the door and down the stairs.

Chapter 6

As Rollie sped away from April's apartment, he called Vivian on his cell phone. "Vivian, we gotta talk," he said when he heard her voice.

"I don't think so, Rollie. We don't have anything to talk about," Vivian said coldly.

"Come on, Vivian—this is crazy! Just because some spiteful girlfriend of yours lied about me, you're totally turned off," Rollie said.

"I've got to go," Vivian said. The dial tone hummed in Rollie's ear.

Within a few seconds, Rollie's cell phone rang. Maybe Vivian had changed her mind! But it was April. She sounded hysterical. "Rollie, I just got a terrible threatening note in the mail! I don't know what to do. Please come right away!"

Rollie turned around and headed back to April's apartment building. When he checked in through security and finally got to April's apartment, she was sitting in a chair crying.

"Where's the note?" he asked.

"It's there on the coffee table. Oh, Rollie, it's *so* awful!" she whimpered.

Rollie quickly read the message. It was composed of letters that had been cut out of magazine and newspaper ads. There was no handwriting to check out.

April Foster:

I love you. If I can't have you, nobody will. You will die.

Your admirer

"Sounds like a real sicko," Rollie said as he examined the envelope. He saw that there was no return address on the back. Someone had even spelled out April's address by pasting letters and numbers together.

"Oh, Rollie, help me! What am I

going to do?" April groaned.

"Well, this is serious enough to call the police. You got a death threat, April. This is no laughing matter," Rollie said.

"But they won't believe me," April wailed.

"They will now. You've got physical evidence in this letter," Rollie said.

"Please don't call the police right away," April said. "Just stay with me and make sure that he can't get me."

"Come on, April, be reasonable. I can hardly be your bodyguard twenty-four hours a day!" Rollie said. "Believe me— now is the time for the police to come in on this."

April curled up until she looked like a little ball in the big chair. "Okay. Call them if you want to. But they won't *do* anything. They'll probably think I'm making it up, just like they did before."

Rollie sat down across from her. "I'll still stay on the case, April, but I'm afraid this is getting dangerous. You really *did* call the police before, didn't you, April? Because my friend's dad checked it out, and he couldn't find any police report—"

"I *told* you they didn't take me seriously. That just proves it! They never even filed a report!" April said. Her eyes grew large and moist. "You know, I think they actually thought I was *crazy*. Uh, I never told you before, Rollie—but right after high school I did some pretty weird stuff. It got so bad that my parents—uh—put me into a hospital. Maybe the police found out about that. That would explain why they don't believe me now."

"No, no," Rollie said. "A lot of kids need counseling. That has nothing to do with what's happening now."

April smiled. "You're terrific, Rollie— you always were. Even when I was Margaret Fierster and all the guys were laughing at me, you were always nice," she said.

Rollie felt ashamed. "No, I wasn't," he thought to himself. "I was laughing right along with the rest of them."

Rollie agreed to hang around the apartment for a while, hoping the stalker might show up. He called David's father and said he needed to quietly check out a threatening note received by an emotionally fragile girl.

But the stalker didn't show up. Late that afternoon April served Rollie some Danish rolls on a pretty plate and offered to brew some coffee.

"Boy, am I ever ready for that," Rollie said, sitting down.

April smiled and went back into the kitchen. A few minutes later she called out to him, "The coffee is almost done, honey."

Rollie stiffened. *Honey?*

Chapter 7

Rollie decided to ignore the term of endearment. Surely, April had just misspoken. But as he drank the coffee and ate the Danish, he noticed that she was staring at him with a strange look on her face. "I really wish you were free to date me," she said. "We could have so much fun together! Is it really *serious* between you and that Vivian?"

Rollie was so tired that he said more than he wanted to say. "Right now she's so mad at me she won't even talk to me. One of her stupid girlfriends saw you and me at Rovers. Now Vivian thinks that we're *dating*—and she's furious at me! Someone told Vivian we were acting real lovey-dovey, and that poisoned her mind. I can't understand why anybody—

let alone a 'friend'—would tell someone such malicious lies."

"Wow, your Vivian must be one of those jealous types. That would be really hard to live with. And you know what they say about people like that. She'll *never* trust you. She's always going to think you're looking at somebody else," April said.

"Maybe. But Vivian was always so cool and sensible. She didn't seem to have a jealous bone in her body. I guess this girl who told her about seeing us in Rovers really told a good story. She said we were hugging and kissing!" Rollie sighed. He was more tired than he could remember being in a long time. Not since he was pulling all-nighters before college exams had he felt so weary.

"Rollie, you look exhausted. Why don't you sleep on the couch here in the living room tonight? You can go home tomorrow morning. I'll go into the bedroom and have my best night's sleep in ages. Just knowing that you're here to protect me really helps me to relax," April said.

"No, I better go home now," Rollie said, starting to get up. But his legs felt like they had just run the last lap of a marathon. "Wow, I *am* beat!"

April hurried to get a blanket. "Just lie down and rest. You can sleep for a couple hours and then go home later if you want to," she said.

Rollie was sorely tempted to stay. He couldn't imagine why he was so sleepy. "Okay," he said, stretching out on the couch. He nodded off in seconds and lapsed into a deep sleep, which wasn't like him. Usually he was a light sleeper. But he didn't awaken until the next morning! When he opened his eyes the first thing he saw was April's beaming face. She was smiling and offering him coffee. "Welcome to the new day, sleepyhead," she said in a soft, seductive voice.

"Man, I went out like a light!" Rollie gasped, staring at his watch. It was already 8:00 A.M.

"It was so great having you spend the night," April said. "I'll tell you a little secret. I pretended that this was the beginning of maybe you and me moving in together."

Rollie gulped down his coffee. Then he looked up. "Look, April, you're a beautiful, wonderful girl—but I'm not interested in a romantic relationship with you. I never could be," he said.

April looked hurt, as if someone had slapped her across the mouth with an open hand. "But—I'm beautiful now. You said so yourself. What more could a guy want? We both know that I never had any dates because I was overweight and unattractive. But now that I'm pretty, I *deserve* you!" she said.

"April, it's not about looks. People want to find friends with personalities that fit their own. It's *not* just looks. I'm in love with Vivian, and she's not half as pretty as you are! It's just that the two of us are on the same wavelength," Rollie explained.

"What? Y-you mean you could never love me?" April cried out in a grief-stricken voice. "N-not *ever*?"

"I *like* you very much, April—and I want to help you. But I'm in love with somebody else, okay?" Rollie started to get up. Suddenly he had a strong suspicion about why he'd become so tired last night. April must have put something in his coffee—a sleeping powder! He had to get out of here as quickly as he could!

April stood up, a strange, glazed look in her eyes. Rollie was stunned to see that she held a pistol in her hand! "Sit down, honey," she said. "Please sit down—before I have to do something bad to you."

Chapter 8

Rollie tried to stay calm. "April," he said in a firm, even voice. "Put the gun away. What are you doing?"

"I can see that you want to run away from me. When I loved you in high school you ran away with Jenny. I understood that—because she was so much prettier than I was. But now *I'm* really pretty. So there's no reason at all for you to leave. I can't let you run away from me again," April said.

Rollie thought fast. "April, you need me on your side. What if the stalker shows up?" he said. "Now put down the gun so I can help you."

April laughed. The grim lines on her face were frightening. "There *isn't* any stalker, silly! I made him up. But I bet you figured that out a few minutes ago, didn't you? I came up with the idea when I found out you worked for a detective agency. Don't you see how clever that was? *I invented the stalker to bring us together*—and it worked just fine! I even telephoned Vivian and told her that her boyfriend was cheating on her with a beautiful young actress. Oh, you can't imagine what lurid details I gave little Vivian. She was crying like a baby!" April said proudly.

Now, finally, Rollie understood everything. It was April who had turned Vivian so completely against him.

"April, give me the gun. You can't keep me here forever," Rollie said. "If you don't give me the gun in five seconds I'm going to yell my head off and rouse all the neighbors."

"That wouldn't do you any good, Rollie. These apartments are soundproof. And the soundproofing works very well. The guys next door told me they play heavy metal music. But I don't even hear it. Anyway—if you yell, I just might shoot you," April said, her voice rising with emotion. "Do you know what it's like when nobody loves you? No, of course you don't—because it's never happened to you! How could you know what I went through as fat, mocked Margaret Fierster?" April's whole body was now writhing with rage.

Rollie was desperate to get away. But he couldn't help feeling sorry for the girl. She must have suffered terribly to have come to this point. "I understand that you're hurt and angry, April—but this isn't the way to handle it," he said in a calm, kind voice. But inside he had a sinking feeling that she would never listen to reason.

"No, you *don't* understand, Rollie. Nobody did! Even my own parents were ashamed of me. I used to hear them talking—my pretty mom and handsome dad. 'How did we get this whale for our daughter?' they'd ask each other. Then they'd blame each other's families. They'd say I took after Mom's sister, tubby Aunt Elsie, or cheerful, chubby Gloria—Dad's cousin. Mom never went anywhere with me. Not even to the mall when other twelve-year-olds went shopping with their moms every Saturday. My parents wouldn't even come to school on parents' night because they were so embarrassed. Ohhh, how I suffered," April said, letting out a pain-filled groan.

"I know it must have been hard, April, but—" Rollie tried to cut in.

"The boys would waddle behind me at the lockers. They'd puff out their cheeks with air or oink like pigs. I pretended not to notice, but I'd always hear the explosion of laughter. Those creeps almost choked laughing. Even my grandma couldn't see beyond the fat. I remember her saying, 'Oh, Margie, why must you be such a pudge?' Then she'd give me a little poke in the stomach and frown," April said.

"April, listen—" Rollie started to say.

"*Shut up, Rollie!*" April snapped. "I thought for sure everything would be different when we got together. For once in my life I'd have a handsome boyfriend who would love me! But no— not even becoming beautiful did the trick. I'm still a loser. It's not *fair* that I still have to suffer!"

"You just need some help, April. You can have a great life, believe me. You're pretty and talented," Rollie said.

"*Help?* Oh, I get it. You think they should send me back to that hospital. No way, Rollie! I hated it there. It's too bad you don't get the picture, Rollie. If you didn't have that creepy Vivian hanging onto you, we'd have a chance. *She's* the real problem. So you need to get rid of her right now, once and for all. Go on— do it! Call Vivian up and tell her that she's ugly, and that you don't want to see her anymore," April demanded.

Rollie could hardly believe what he was hearing. His mind went blank. "April, I can't do that," he gasped.

"Well then, maybe *I'll* call Vivian. Yeah, that ought to work. I'll tell her you've had an accident and you need her. Then when she shows up, I'll have to do something bad to her. Is *that* what you want, Rollie?" April snarled.

Chapter 9

"Okay, okay," Rollie said. "I'll call Vivian. And I'll tell her whatever you want. Just keep her away from here."

"Oh, my, that's so touching," April sneered bitterly. "I'm really impressed to see how much you care about her and want to protect her. How come nobody ever felt that way about *me*?"

"Somebody will if you just give them a chance, April," Rollie pleaded. "Look, put the gun away and—"

April brought the phone over and set it on the table in front of Rollie. "Okay, it's time to call Vivian now. You know what to say. Tell her she's ugly, and that she was always a dog. Say you have a pretty girlfriend now and don't need her. You better tell her every word of that," she said. "I'm going to be standing right here listening. So if you try to signal her that something is wrong, you'll be in big trouble."

Rollie's body was dripping with sweat, but he didn't know what else to do. "Okay," he agreed. He punched out Vivian's number and the phone rang several times before she answered. He'd been hoping she was out, so he'd get her machine—but no such luck.

"Hello?" Vivian said.

"Vivian? It's me," Rollie said nervously, "and I—uh—just wanted to tell you that—" April waved the gun at him threateningly and he continued, "Well, you're ugly, Vivian, and you know you've always been a dog, and I've got a new girlfriend, and she's really beautiful, so I don't need you anymore."

Vivian didn't answer right away. When she did speak, she sounded shaken. "What's the matter with you, Rollie? Are you drunk, or what?"

April shook her head. Rollie knew what he had to do. He had to convince Vivian that he was stone cold sober and telling her exactly how he felt.

"No, Vivian, I'm sober. This is how I really feel about you. I just thought it was important to tell the truth about what I think," Rollie said.

"Rollie, what is it? You sound weird. Is something wrong? Has something happened to you?" Vivian demanded. "Where are you? The way you're talking is scaring me. It's not like you—"

April scowled at Rollie. Her lips silently mouthed the demand, "You have to *make* her believe you. Do it now—I'm warning you!"

"Vivian, just forget about me. I don't love you anymore, okay? Just forget I ever existed," Rollie said.

April mouthed the words, "Tell her to drop dead, and then hang up."

Rollie's heart ached, but he said, "Vivian, drop dead!" Then he slammed down the receiver with a bang.

April rocked back on her heels and broke out laughing. "Ohhhh, can you imagine what she's thinking right now? She must feel like she's been dragged through a dunghill! Well, that's too bad, because it's her turn now! That's the way I've felt all my life! That's *exactly* what life for Margaret Fierster was like.

"Do you get it now? That's why I decided to become someone else. So I dieted and exercised and worked myself into exhaustion in order to be beautiful. After doing all that, I was sure I could have the guy I loved.

"But you know what?" April gripped the gun and gave Rollie a fierce look. "I was rejected again—can you believe it? I was dragged through the dunghill *again*. When is it going to stop? Tell me, Rollie, when am I supposed to get *my* turn?" Her voice rose to a frightening fever pitch.

Chapter 10

Rollie felt sick and scared. Back in high school he had never given a moment's thought to what Margaret Fierster was going through. And not just her. There were quite a few "Margarets" in his class. There was the lanky guy who had a bad complexion—the one they called "the zit pole." And how about the little shrimp who looked like an eighth-grader even when he was a senior? Guys would pick him up like a baby to make him feel even smaller. There was the kid from Russia who talked funny, and the clueless airheads who got bad grades.

Now it all came back to him very clearly. Rollie could remember all the laughs the *in crowd* got from teasing the kids they considered losers. Margaret wasn't the only one. Now he felt terribly sorry—but it was too late.

"Margaret, I'm truly sorry that I wasn't nicer to you. And I'm sorry for not understanding how you felt. It was cruel. But you can have a good life *now*. I'll help you, Margaret," Rollie said.

"I'm *not* Margaret!" she shrieked at him. "Don't call me Margaret. The whale is dead. And April Foster will be dead pretty soon, too—but that's okay, because you will, too. At least we'll be together. When nobody loves you, what's the sense of living?"

"Look, April, we're still *young* people! We've got plenty to live for," Rollie cried out desperately.

Then Rollie watched in horror as she grasped the pistol with both hands and got ready to fire. He couldn't wait. So he lunged at her, counting on the fact that she probably wasn't a crack shot. She wasn't. The bullet went wild, crashing into the ceiling and sending down a shower of plaster. Then Rollie grabbed the gun and April fell, sobbing, to the floor.

Rollie held the gun on her as he called the police. Then he tried to comfort the sobbing girl. "It's not as hopeless as you think. All of those awful experiences just messed up your mind, April." She didn't say a word until the police knocked on the door. Then she spoke in a soft, flat voice. "All I ever wanted was for people to like me—"

After watching the patrol car drive off, Rollie sped over to Vivian's dorm. He couldn't imagine what she must be thinking about now.

Vivian wasn't in her room, but her roommate directed Rollie to the library. There she was, sitting on the grassy knoll in front of the library. She held an open book on her lap, but Rollie could see that she wasn't reading. Her eyes were puffy and red from crying.

Rollie approached her cautiously. "Vivi, it's me," he said softly.

Vivian looked up at him. "Are you all right?" she asked.

"Oh, Vivi, I was working on this case for a very disturbed lady. She made up a bogus story about a stalker. When I called you, she was aiming a gun at me. She *forced* me to say those terrible things," Rollie explained.

Vivian smiled a little. "I knew you were too nice a guy to talk to me like that—even if we were breaking up," she said. Then she jumped up and ran to him. "Rollie, I'm so sorry I didn't trust you," she whispered as she put her arms around him.

Rollie hugged her tightly. "The girl I was trying to help—she's the one who called you with that stupid story, Vivi. She had a crazy romantic fantasy about me. That's why she wanted to break us up. Somehow she imagined that she and I would get together," Rollie said.

Vivian drew back, her gaze searching Rollie's face. "Was she an old girlfriend or something? I mean—like, were you guys ever in love?" she asked.

"No, no, nothing like that!" Rollie said. "When we were in high school I didn't even like her. I never even gave her a kind word." Then he felt a wave of sadness wash over him, and he added, "Nobody did."

"I love you," Vivian whispered.

"And I love you too, babe," Rollie answered. Then, as he closed his eyes and kissed her, he felt a rush of gratitude. How lucky he was to hear the blessed words that no one had ever spoken to Margaret Fierster.

COMPREHENSION QUESTIONS

RECALL

1. Why didn't Rollie recognize his old classmate?

2. Why did Vivian get so angry with Rollie?

3. What emotion did Rollie feel when he thought about Margaret Fierster?

ANALYZING CHARACTERS

1. What two words could describe Rollie? Explain your thinking.
   - *ambitious*
   - *heartless*
   - *faithful*

2. What two words could describe Vivian Garcia? Tell why you think so.
   - *unreliable*
   - *forgiving*
   - *disappointed*

DRAWING CONCLUSIONS

1. Why was Rollie unable to find April's stalker?

2. Why did April think she "deserved" a relationship with Rollie?

3. What kind of "help" did April *not* want?

VOCABULARY

1. April said she "followed a strict daily regimen to keep the weight off." What is a *regimen*?

2. April went to a "cattle call" for a new musical production. What is a *cattle call*?

3. April sounded "hysterical" when she told Rollie about the threatening note. What does *hysterical* mean?